CHRISTINA
JAMES

Saving

Christmas

This is a work of fiction. Names, characters, places and incidents are either the product of the author's imagination or are used fictitiously. Any resemblance to actual persons living or dead, business establishments, events, or locales, is entirely coincidental.

Saving Christmas

Published by Valerie Harris
Copyright 2012 by Valerie Harris
Cover by Angela Anderson, Angela Anderson Design
Layout by www.formatting4U.com
ISBN: 978-1-938799-13-6

Previously published by The Wild Rose Press under *Saving Christmas by Christina James.*

Dedication

To my children, Courtney and Scott, my pride and joy.

Chapter One

Doug Brophy couldn't believe his eyes as he walked into his office at Shelby Police Station. His fellow officers had decorated the place like it was Santa's Village or something. Garland strung from corner to corner, stockings with glittered names hung on one wall, a table top Christmas tree dressed in blinking lights adorned a desk.

Jeez, am I the only one working around here?

"Who the hell would kidnap Santa a week before Christmas?" Officer Lane shouted to no one in particular.

A group of officers and detectives gathered around the TV watching a developing news story. Doug barely caught a glimpse of the reporter as he passed the group. Whatever it was he didn't care unless it was his apartment on fire or a missing kid. He had enough to worry about.

"Brophy, come check this out. It ain't right when even Santa Claus ain't safe," Officer Marlin said. "And in broad daylight, too." The older man shook his head while he sat with a hip slung over the corner of a desk. "Goddamn shame."

Doug ignored the invite, strode to his desk, and

plopped in his chair preparing to tackle the mountain of paperwork piled high in front of him. He had no time to watch the noontime news. Hell, Shelby, Oregon may not be a bustling place like New York or Boston, but it had its share of troubles just like any mid-sized town sandwiched between two bigger cities and with access to a major highway. If he stopped to look at the news every time a crime happened, he'd never leave the front of the TV.

With the arrest of a suspect in his last case, Doug now had reports due to the DA's office by morning. Not to mention the countless other reports awaiting his attention. So he left the gawking to his fellow officers.

He shuffled files around and sighed, not knowing where to start. If he weren't buried constantly in endless reports, he could be back on the street following leads to his open cases instead of wasting time pushing a pen. When his partner, Erik, who had been stabbed by a suspect, returned from injury leave, Doug planned a major guilt trip for the guy, along with some shit for causing him to worry. He made a mental note to call him and check up on his recovery.

"Detective Brophy," Lt. Caldwell bellowed, rushing into the room, still agile at sixty-years-old. "The kidnapping at the Melway Mall has all the markings of a press nightmare, not to mention a political backlash." He twisted to point at the TV then turned back to Doug. "Those damn reporters got to the scene within minutes of the first responding officers so now it's impossible to prevent the firestorm of public panic those idiots created once they went live with Santa's kidnapping."

Normally, Lt. Caldwell was calm and unflappable. With him this fired up, Doug grew uncomfortable.

"Brophy, I'm pulling you from your current cases and placing you as Lead Detective on this kidnapping. Now go save Christmas."

Yup, Doug didn't like the vibes one bit.

Aw, shit! I'll never get any work done with this kind of interruption.

Doug stood and faced the lieutenant. "Yes, sir. Who's working with me?"

"That's got to be obvious. Whoever you damn well need! Didn't you just hear a word I said? This is a political nightmare. Santa gets kidnapped a week before Christmas. Haven't you watched one bit of the coverage from the scene?" Lt. Caldwell thumbed over his shoulder, his eyes set in a deep frown.

Officer Marlin spoke up. "Lieutenant, I tried to get his ass over here, but he wouldn't listen. This is Santa Claus we're talking about, Brophy."

The last thing Doug needed was the mocking tone Marlin shared. Oh, his fellow officers were sure to bust his balls forever on this case, especially if he couldn't get the missing Santa back.

"Will someone please share the details instead of busting my balls?" Doug hollered around the room.

Lieutenant Caldwell stood by Doug's desk with his arms crossed. "About half an hour ago at approximately eleven thirty this morning, a van pulled up outside the Melway Mall. Santa Claus was ringing a bell at the front entrance and greeting children who gathered there from a local elementary school to do some Christmas caroling. Three armed men jumped out and grabbed him."

Great! Kids witnessing Santa Claus receiving a beat down. Just great!

"Santa was roughed up while a struggle with the men ensued. Within seconds, the gunmen threw Santa into the van and drove off amongst the screams and cries of the panicked crowd, which consisted primarily of second graders. No one could lend assistance because of the guns and all of the adults scrambled to protect the children. It was all over in under a minute."

Doug drew a deep breath. No one should mess with Santa Claus. "Okay. I'm on it. I'll head to the scene. Marlin, work on getting me Santa's identity and anything you can find out about him."

"Will do," Marlin replied and picked up a phone.

"The police at the scene have been interviewing bystanders," Lt. Caldwell continued to update Doug as they walked from the precinct to the parking lot behind the building.

The sun shone brightly against the partly cloudy sky but the wind whipped through Doug's coat to give a chill that went deep into the bones. With temps in the upper twenties, the snow drifts dotting the curbs would not be shrinking any time soon.

"The Mayor's Office is already sending their Chief Public Relations Officer to meet you there. She'll probably be on scene before you arrive."

Oh, hell no! "That won't be necessary, sir," Doug spoke, trying not to plead or be too obvious in his objection. He knew who the officer was and he sure as hell wanted to steer clear of her. He couldn't admit to anyone just how big of an apology he owed her but somehow he couldn't find the right words—words so she'd understand. "I'll get more done without any interference from a non-law enforcement agency."

Lt. Caldwell grimaced. "Brophy, are you forgetting

who signs our damn checks? That's right. The mayor. And I already told you this case is a political nightmare. I have no say in this matter. The mayor made his decision to have her handle the media and I'm not disobeying him. The mayor's worried about being named the town where Santa disappeared."

"Santa's a figment of the imagination, sir," Doug argued, bewildered at the way everyone kept talking of the man like he really existed. "There is no real Santa."

"Yeah, maybe to you and me. But children all over the world believe in Santa so don't forget that. When fifty children witness Santa's kidnapping…well, there goes Christmas unless we can get him back."

"So, we go on the news, for the kids' sake." Doug shrugged his shoulders. "We could announce Santa has been saved, is back at the North Pole being nursed back to health by Mrs. Claus, and will be ready for Christmas."

Lt. Caldwell stepped closer. "Don't get wise with me, Brophy. You've been mopping around here for months, sour faced, temper like a bear. Maybe it'd do you some good to believe in something like Santa— anything to stop you from being such a miserable fuck." The lieutenant narrowed his eyes. "And there's no way to fake a rescue of Santa, not with all the media coverage. What happens if someone discovers Santa dead on a sidewalk somewhere, the victim of a homicide, huh? We try to lie about his safe return and we can all kiss our careers goodbye. I ain't ready to do that. Now get out there, do some real police work and fucking save Christmas. I chose you for a reason, Brophy."

Doug needed this conversation to end before he froze his ass off. "Why's that?"

Lt. Caldwell spoke slowly, his face more relaxed now. "Because you're a damn good detective and from the info trickling in from the scene, this case has all the makings of a real doozey. I trust your instincts and police work. Don't let me down. You have the Shelby Police Department at your call—use them."

The lieutenant turned and stomped back around the side of the building, disappearing from sight.

Doug entered his unmarked vehicle and let out the sigh that had been building inside him. Working in the same town for local government agencies, it was inevitable he'd run into the mayor's spokesperson again. Why did it have to be now when he was preoccupied with this case and unable to collect his thoughts? He knew he needed to make things right with her, he just wasn't sure how.

He turned on the vehicle's blue lights, and with his siren blaring, peeled out of the parking lot, weaving past traffic as it pulled over to allow him passage. Part of him didn't want to admit that he was rushing to the crime scene for more than just the case.

Jesus, not only did he have to find Santa so that Christmas wouldn't be ruined for children everywhere, but he also had to protect himself. Protect his heart from one very sexy and smart Chief Public Relations Officer, who probably wanted to see his head on a platter more than she wanted to see Santa rescued.

Only time would tell.

Chapter Two

Doug didn't need to be a detective to figure out Paulina Smithfield was probably plotting revenge and his family jewels might just be her target. It didn't matter that she had a sweet smile plastered on her lovely face or that she was dressed in a form fitting navy-blue business skirt and jacket which was both sexy and professional. Her short, black, wool coat was unbuttoned allowing Doug a view of the slender curves he remembered all too well.

It didn't matter that she looked calm and sure.

All that mattered was how her crystal blue eyes darkened to a cool shade of dark blue when she noticed him standing beside her in front of the Melway Mall entrance. The familiar slap of lust hit him the moment he set eyes on the leggy brunette, her long hair swept up in a neat bun. Her creamy skin was flawless, her beauty evident even when wearing little makeup. Her soft vanilla scent had him taking a discreet deep breath.

Big eyes stared at him now that Paulina had angled her head up to look at him. He admired her ability to mask her emotions with what must've been years of training to remain cool under pressure.

But Paulina couldn't fool Doug. He could tell her temper simmered under that cool demeanor and would let him have it if they were in private. Not only the change in her eye color warned him but the way her breasts heaved up then down, faster and faster since he had stepped beside her.

"Detective Brophy, so glad to have you on this case," Paulina said losing her smile.

Doug wished he was anywhere but here. *God, she must hate me.* "Anything I can do to resolve this quickly—you have my word I'll do just that."

She crossed her arms. "And we know what your word means, don't we, Detective Brophy?"

Ouch! Doug cringed inwardly praying she'd keep her claws to herself. But he had to admit, seeing this feisty side of her was an instant turn on. Oh hell, why was he even daring to think like this again?

"Any new developments?" Doug asked, opening his notebook. It was best to change the subject and keep it professional. With any luck, this would be over before he had to explain that fateful night to Paulina.

"Follow me, Detective." Paulina turned on stiletto heels that showcased long, toned legs, forever etched in his memories.

He wanted to groan at the recollection. If there was a medal for being a dumb ass, he'd be awarded it for past behavior. Walking behind her presented him the view of her hot ass. The curves beneath that layer of fabric made his mouth water. *Stop it!* He shouldn't go down that path again.

"You know, Paulina, you can call me Doug. No need for formalities."

She stopped so fast that he walked into her, his

hands automatically grasping her hips. His fingers begged to knead the soft skin he knew lay beneath that suit.

Before he had the chance, Paulina removed his hands and turned. "Let's get one thing straight, *Doug*," she said in a whisper between clenched teeth. "We're only talking because we have to. Otherwise, what I have to say, you really wouldn't want to hear."

Okay, I deserve that. "It was your office that placed you on this case with me. I'm not here to make you uncomfortable, Paulina."

"Too late for that. Let's just get back to work." Without another word, she walked in the opposite direction leaving Doug no choice but to follow.

Paulina waltzed through a large door and into the mall. She walked quickly to a hallway and through another door. "Doug, this is the security center for the entire mall. I'm sure you'll want to review the videotape they recovered from the entrance. It caught the entire kidnapping on tape...well, everything except when they threw Santa in the van."

"Really?" Doug stepped further into the room, studying the array of monitors displaying different locations throughout the mall. The command center boasted new technology that even the police didn't have yet. The clarity on the videos should provide a decent picture of the perps. "It's rare to get such a break in a case. We usually don't get a bird's eye view of the suspects. With any luck, we can use the media to circulate the images and set up a tip line. Show me what you got?"

A security guard pressed a few buttons and the screen came to life showing Santa happily shaking a bell one minute, and in the next, he was in the fight of his life with three gunmen. There wasn't a view of the perimeter of the entrance, but through the doorways, they could see Santa being dragged from where he was standing to the van and then out of view of the cameras. Doug's heart sank when he saw the group of small children standing in the background watching the whole scene unfold before their scared little eyes. Some cried. Others huddled together. *Son of a bitch!* Had one of those assholes fired a shot, they could've hit any number of small kids.

"Any chance one of your cameras, anywhere on the premise, got the van's plate number?" Doug asked, hoping for another great break in a very weird case. Who was bold enough to attempt a kidnapping of such a famed figure in the middle of the day with throngs of witnesses around?

"No, sir," the security guard responded. "The only view from the cameras is on the entrances and not further into the parking lot where the van pulled up along the fire lane."

"But a bystander recorded half of the license plate number," said a Shelby officer who was already in the room when Doug and Paulina arrived. "Bad news is that the digits match three plates in the system and one plate comes back stolen. The other two come back to sedans."

Doug shook his head and crossed his arms. "Damn it. Any chance of getting some good news to share?"

"Yes, sir," the police officer said, flipping through his notebook. "The kidnapped Santa is identified as Peter Howlings. He's been employed here the last two weeks, now that the holiday shopping season is in full swing. He worked as Santa four days a week. No disciplinary problems. But a criminal record check shows convictions for drug dealing and petty theft. A further look into his record revealed an active warrant for his arrest as part of a local gang's drug bust. Howlings was the only perp to flee the scene and has yet to be picked up. Out ran the arresting officers."

"And yet he was able to get hired as Santa at a mall? Who in the hell hires a convict to play Santa to thousands of innocent kids?" Doug demanded from everyone just as a man dressed in a dark business suit stepped into the room.

"I'm sorry," Paulina interjected, flashing a wild glare at Doug. "Doug, this is General Manager, Henry Pattins. What Detective Brophy is trying to say is that a criminal record check would've ensured Mr. Howlings not be hired with his criminal past, isn't that right?" she asked of the new man standing off to her side.

"Well, yes, of course—" the man began before Doug cut him off.

"Don't tell me what I'm trying to say, Paulina," Doug said with heat. "The Mayor's Office won't dictate how I run this investigation." Doug focused his attention on Henry. "Mr. Pattins, it's damn absurd that the man was allowed to work here at all. By not running a background check, all customers and employees were put at risk. For all you know, you were putting a drug pusher or a sexual predator out there to prey on these children. What do you want for Christmas, little Ricky?" Doug mocked and didn't care if he pissed off the world. "Why, Santa, I want a bag of coke and some crack."

The room remained silent. Doug could feel

Paulina's glare heating his skin. "Look, I don't give a damn about political correctness right now. Kids were placed in serious jeopardy today because someone forgot to do a simple background check that could've prevented this entire event from happening. What do you expect when you hire known criminals?"

The other man cleared his throat and spoke. "As General Manager of this mall, Detective Brophy, I can assure you we do background checks on all of our employees."

"Seems like you forgot one," Doug replied.

"Doug, would you let the man speak?" Paulina demanded.

"What I mean is that it takes some time to get the records back. With the holiday season, we were pressed for time and hired Mr. Howlings with the understanding that any blips on his record would be grounds for firing."

"You fools," Doug scolded. "Don't you think Howlings knew that the season would be over before you'd ever find out the truth about him? Criminals know how bogged down the system is and they know how to take full advantage of it."

"Yes, I know that now," the man conceded. "I can assure you we'll be changing our hiring procedures effective immediately."

"It's a shame that it takes a crime before people wise up to what needs to be changed," Doug commented. "Get me print-outs of all the video shots ASAP. Run the tread again." Doug studied the video. "Stop. Print this still for distribution to the press. And only this shot gets out. Do not release these video clips to the press. Understood, Mr. Pattins?"

Henry nodded. "Of course, Detective Brophy. Melway Mall plans to fully cooperate with all law enforcement agencies. Whatever we can do, we'll do it."

Doug bit his tongue knowing he had said all that was necessary. He turned and left the room, but the sound of heels clacking against the marble floor told him Paulina followed.

"You can stop any time, you know," Paulina said.

Doug halted and faced her. "You shouldn't have tried to put words in my mouth, Paulina."

"And you need to remember the sensitivity of this case."

Doug stood his ground, hands on his hips, looking down into those dazzling, light blue eyes. "Give me a break. Our victim is a drug dealer. No wait. Not just any drug dealer—a convicted one. A criminal with a warrant for fleeing a drug bust. So excuse me if I don't feel bad for the kidnapped Santa."

Doug stomped off, refusing to be reprimanded by the voice of the Mayor's Office. Walking outside, the cold afternoon air did nothing to deflate the temper spiraling through him. He hated drug dealers.

"Hey, mista," a young voice sounded and a small hand tugged on Doug's sleeve. When he looked down, big blue eyes stared up at him, tears staining the little boy's cheeks.

Doug bent down to be eye level with the kid. "What is it, son?"

"You have a badge on your belt and a gun so you must be a cop, right?"

"Yes, I am."

"Then you've just got to save Santa Claus. Those

13

men were really mean to him. They hurt him. Do you think he's dead?" His voice trembled with each word.

Oh, Christ. Doug could use a stiff drink right about now. How could he reassure this kid who was obviously traumatized by the events of the day? A slender shadow came from behind, darkening the sidewalk in front of him. A quick peak over his shoulder showed Paulina had followed him outside. Great! Just what he needed—to be caught being sympathetic in front of the one woman who probably wished him dead.

"Look, little man, what happened today will be cleared up real soon, okay? The police help people who run into some trouble, like Santa."

"Uh-uh. Santa didn't do anything wrong. He wasn't running anywhere. He was standing right there when that van pulled up and took him."

"I'm sorry, officer. My son has had a rough day," a man said from behind the boy.

Doug glanced up. "Not a problem. I'm sure he's still very upset."

"Without Santa, how can there be Christmas?" the boy exclaimed, tears gathering in his eyes again. Behind them another group of kids were standing watching while their parents talked to each other.

Doug needed damage control and fast. "Um, this here is my friend, Paulina. She works for the Mayor's Office," he said, standing and grabbing Paulina's elbow with a gentle motion. He tugged her beside him. "She's helping me find Santa and can answer all of your questions."

Paulina's voice was as gentle as Doug had ever heard it as she spoke to the little boy and his father.

"Now don't you worry about Santa. He's got magic behind him. Why I bet right now he's telling those naughty men they had better write a long letter saying they're sorry or they won't get any Christmas presents this year."

"They don't deserve presents," the boy exclaimed, a pout framing his chubby face.

"No. They don't, that's for sure. But I know Santa will be found in plenty of time to celebrate Christmas. Now you know what you can do?"

"What?"

"You should go home and write Santa a letter. I'm sure he'll love to read it once he gets back home. Detective Brophy here is very good at finding people. And he will have Santa home for Christmas. You'll see."

"Come on, son," the boy's father said, cupping his shoulders. "Thank you both. We'll write that letter as soon as we get home."

The pair disappeared into the crowd.

"Christ, Paulina, do you have to make me out to be some miracle worker?" Doug complained into her ear. He regretted getting so close to her once her perfume took hold of his senses and shot a lust-filled lightning bolt straight to his cock. Getting a hard-on in public was bad enough, but while searching for Santa? Shit, he was losing it.

"Thought it would keep you focused if you had a fan club," Paulina said, her smile welcomed. But was it meant to be a truce?

"Never slacked on the job even if I don't always go about things the right way." His breath hitched for a brief moment, remembering his past blunder. "I'll

15

catch up with you later. Good seeing you. It really was," Doug admitted, a dull ache in his chest warned him she was quicksand and dragging him in quickly. "See ya."

Paulina shouted at his back. "Doug?" He turned to face her as she walked up to him. "I'm sorry if you were misinformed, but we're partners until this case is resolved. So it's not goodbye, although I do appreciate you having the decency to say goodbye this time."

And here it comes. "Um, yeah, about that."

She put her palm up in front of his face. "Save it, stud. Not interested in boring excuses for pitiful behavior. Let's get back to work. What's the next move?"

"Next move?" *So she doesn't want an explanation for breaking things off with her six months ago? I can live with that.*

Buttoning her jacket, she didn't look at him. "Where do we go from here? What's the next part of the investigation?"

"Well, since we know who the victim is, we'll start at his favorite watering hole. One of my officers texted me the info so we'll start there. Then we'll stop by the precinct, pull the file and dig into his past. Got to warn you, it won't be pretty."

"Listen, don't try to scare me off. Working in the Mayor's Office, I'm privy to everything that happens in this city—more so than you, Doug. I'm not a delicate flower that's going to wilt at the first sign of trouble. You should know that by now. You're driving since I got dropped off here." She didn't wait for his response but sauntered past him toward his vehicle.

This case could turn out to be very interesting.

Chapter Three

It was bad enough Santa was missing and wreaking havoc on children everywhere, but did Paulina have to be in such close vicinity with the man who shredded her heart six months ago?

I can do this, she lectured herself in the solitude of the undercover cop car Doug fueled up. She had gotten over Doug months ago, forced herself to see him for the loser he was instead of the sexy, down-to-earth guy she had grown to care about.

But seeing him try to help the little boy today had given her second thoughts that maybe he wasn't the loser she wanted to believe he was. Even though she could tell he wanted to offer her an explanation today, but she hadn't wanted to hear the truth behind why he had stopped calling her, stopped taking her calls. She feared the truth, feared him telling her she didn't appeal to him. But when they had kissed while dating it was explosive, like nothing she had ever experienced before. Had she read too much into it? She couldn't even say he used her for sex because they had never made it to bed, just heavy petting and kissing. He had held back. Maybe he wasn't attracted to her after all. Oh, how she wished she wasn't attracted to him.

"Oh, oh." Doug said, climbing back into the car and driving off. "A woman deep in thought is scary. What are you thinking?"

She only shrugged, wishing someone else could've been assigned to work with him. "Just trying to organize my thoughts is all. You have to admit, Doug, it's been a busy afternoon. Just trying to take it all in."

Glancing at him was a mistake. The sharp angles of his face beckoned her knuckles to stroke across. The dark blue eyes set under long lashes promised dreamy stares. Short sandy brown hair had her fingers curling as she thought about running them through it. And those lips...they were made for kissing. All of it reminded her he was the one man she couldn't have. Because he hadn't wanted her.

The jerk!

"You're sure you don't want me to swing you by your place to at least change your shoes, Paulina?"

"No, thank you. I'm fine." If he thought he'd be invited to come anywhere close to her house, he was sorely mistaken.

"Okay. Your call. We're going to be doing a lot of walking around Shelby today and it's cold and slippery out. Sidewalks may be shoveled from the snowstorm the other day but sure ain't weather for walking in heels."

She gritted her teeth, not needing his concern. "I said I'm fine."

Now why did he need to look so damn desirable when he frowned like that? She sighed and chose to stare out the passenger window while he drove through town to a bar frequented by Peter Howlings, a.k.a. Santa Claus, MIA.

"If you say so." His fingers toyed with the radio station, stopping on a rock-and-roll tune, before tapping the steering wheel to the beat.

The car ride reminded her of the dates they had enjoyed months ago. He wore the same damn cologne too, subtle but enough to tickle her nose with its woodsy scent. Always relaxed and confident, he had enjoyed music back then too, keeping the mood light and refreshing. With a soft sigh, she watched the neighborhoods speed by.

Looking back to those lost months, she still couldn't figure out where they went wrong. Maybe she was just too busy with her demanding job, always making him wait for her to get out of a meeting or an appointment that ran longer than expected. But he never seemed to mind, always greeting her with a smile.

Or was it the way she would debate any topic she believed in until she was hoarse? That, too, didn't appear to have an adverse effect on him. Hadn't he laughed when she had argued her point until he called a truce? Even going as far as pointing out it was a sexy attribute.

His dumping her could've been because of her lack of availability to plan a romantic weekend get-a-way even though they had discussed it several times. Oh, there were so many maybes. It would've been nice to hear from him which one it was. And now she was afraid to hear what it was, not wanting to live through the embarrassment.

How did she make anyone understand that her career was important and she still needed to prove herself as a newcomer in city hall? That took a lot of time and energy. She had always tried to make the best of her personal time, hadn't she?

Her responsibilities had become so immense that many things in her life had taken a backseat. Her heart pounded with a series of short thuds. Or had she done that when Doug stopped calling as a way to forget him? She didn't remember working this hard when dating Doug. Could be that working was the only thing keeping her from any more self-doubts on her failure with him.

She swallowed hard as Doug pulled into the parking lot of a dilapidated one-story wooden building. The name outside read *Charlie's Rack 'em and Stack 'em* in faded red letters.

"Be sure to stay close to me in here. This place doesn't welcome strangers or police with open arms. And let me do the talking," Doug said, without waiting for her to respond.

Who does he think he is giving one order after another? "Fine. Just remember the sensitivity of the case." Easing out of the car, she stepped beside him and walked. "Would've been a better plan to bring along backup...or maybe your brother."

He frowned at her. "What the hell for? I'm a police officer, armed with knowledge and a gun. Don't need my big brother for a routine interrogation, even if his Special Ops ass can be beneficial sometimes, which he's always willing to brag about by the way."

Paulina smiled, remembering meeting the brother once while she dated Doug. Two brothers more the same than either wanted to admit and both living life to help others. She shook the memory from her head, not needing to be sentimental where Doug was concerned.

When they stopped at the entrance, he spoke quietly. "Normally, I'd be a gentleman and hold the door open for you. But not this time. I'm going in first."

The wind whipped at her exposed legs, her nylons adding no protection against the elements. "Then get inside. I'm freezing."

When he shot her an 'I-told-you-so' look, she wanted to choke him but didn't get the chance when he ventured inside. She clung to his side without touching him. The air reeked of stale tobacco and something sour. The lighting was poor but by the looks of the bedraggled customers, sitting over their drinks like they could fall over at any time, it was better not to see them in full light.

Doug strode to the bar like he owned the place. Paulina had to admire his macho stance. She was reminded of what had attracted her to the detective when they met at City Hall that long ago day—the way he carried himself, proud and sure but not arrogant. He had smiled and it lit up the room, made her knees shake for the first time in her life. That morning was the first time she had ever been aroused simply by a man's presence, by the way Doug strutted by.

But that was long ago. She was with him now only because her job called on her to do so. When you worked for the leader of a city, refusing an assignment wasn't possible, especially when there were so many others waiting in the background to jump into her shoes. She hadn't spent years sacrificing her social life to work the long hours on the campaign trail, mingling in the political circuit, and finishing her master's degree with night courses to throw it all away just because she didn't like the man she'd been assigned to work with.

This wasn't the first time Paulina loathed a part of her job, but it was the first time she felt so damn vulnerable. Trying to convince herself that there was no longer an attraction between her and Doug was as draining as the demands of her twelve-hour schedule.

"Well, don't get you fancy types in here too often," the bartender snarled. "Must be fucking fuzz. Where's your badge, officer?"

Doug didn't flinch. He merely whipped out his credentials and put them away just as fast, giving the man only a glance at them.

"That piece of metal don't mean shit to me. What are you drinking?"

Doug smirked. "Didn't come for a social visit, asshole. Came to ask some questions."

The guy took a long drag of his cigarette and blew it in Doug's direction. Paulina lost all braveness and wanted to get the hell out of there before they disappeared like Santa. But Doug remained cool.

Daring to peek around the room, she noticed some people watching them. Feeling uncomfortable, Paulina turned her attention back to Doug and the man behind the bar, hoping he'd cooperate so they could leave.

"You don't buy a drink, I don't answer any fucking questions. I'm making a living here. Not talking." The guy roamed Paulina's body, licking his lips. "Why don't you let me get you a drink, sugar? Haven't seen a fine woman like you in here. Bet you shave your pussy all nice and clean."

Paulina's skin crawled with disgust. Her gasp had been loud.

Doug reached across the bar, and with one arm, grabbed the man by the collar of his shirt and dragged him halfway over the bar. "Apologize to the lady—*now*. Or you'll be picking your balls off the fucking floor." Doug shook the man and squeezed harder.

Paulina's heart skipped a beat at the intensity of Doug's defense. How could he make her feel so special and so miserable at the same time?

"S-sorry."

"Good. Now tell me what you know about Peter Howlings." Doug shoved a picture in front of the bartender's face, refusing to release his grip on him.

"Get the fuck off me. I know nothing."

Doug shook him harder. His strength was admirable.

"All right...you know guys get killed for talking," the guy conceded, coughing. "He comes in mostly Thursdays and Fridays. Has his share of drinks and leaves."

"Is that before or after he supplies your fine customers with their daily fix?" Doug asked, glaring at another man who walked past them.

The bartender gritted his teeth. "I told you I don't know nothin'. I don't like the damn drugs, but if someone brings them in here without me knowing, then how the fuck am I supposed to stop them?"

Paulina wished she had taken those karate classes her sister had asked her to last year, or at least continued with the kick boxing lessons she took in college. What if this guy got the better of Doug? What the hell would she do, unarmed and untrained for physical combat?

"Gee, I don't know. Maybe call the cops, asshole," Doug said and threw him backward, letting his grip go. "Who did Howlings hang with? Don't fuck with me. I can have fifty cops down here in a heartbeat to tear this place apart and search everyone on premise. Bet that'll kill business for a good while, at least long enough to put you out of business."

Paulina held the office keys in her coat pocket, her only weapon if Doug became disabled and she was left to defend herself.

The man cursed. "He hung with some guy called The Player. I swear that's the only name I ever heard. He liked to play with the women. Dude was out of his element here though."

Doug crossed his arms. "How so?"

The man looked around before speaking. "Always came in dressed nicely. Look around. He stuck out like a sore thumb. But I swear I know nothing about him. He never caused trouble and tipped well. Had plenty of ladies too. Hell, there wasn't a broad in the place who wouldn't do exactly as he asked."

"Seems to me that when a man gets a reputation like that, someone's bound to know more about him. Now why don't you point me in that direction, huh?"

"He wasn't here last week, but come in this Thursday or Friday 'cuz he usually never misses a night. Believe me, you won't miss him. He sticks out like a sore thumb. Pete was the only one I ever saw with him. I doubt the women even know his name, just looking for his money."

Doug gave the man his business card. "Anything else you remember, call me."

Paulina may love her job and want to keep it, but there was no way in hell she'd ever give that sleaze ball her contact info.

Doug grasped Paulina's elbow and walked her quickly outside. The strong touch stirred butterflies in her belly as memories of his kisses filled her mind. She hated her body for its quick reaction. Without a word, he opened the door and helped her inside.

Clearing her throat, she swallowed hard, not sure what unnerved her more—the creepy bar or Doug's closeness. "Tomorrow I'll wear sneakers…in case I have to run," Paulina announced when Doug pulled onto the street.

His laughter filled the car. Why it put her at ease, she couldn't say but it did.

"I say we call it a day for now," Doug said, the smell of cigarettes clinging to their clothes. "Tomorrow I start at seven. When can I expect you?"

"Seven," she said, never wanting to take a shower as bad as she did now. She felt dirty after being in that bar.

They drove in silence until they reached her house.

"You remembered where I lived," she said, sarcasm etched in her tone, pretty shocked that he would but, then again, he was a police officer. And he had been here quite a few times.

"Never forgot, Paulina." The pain in his voice seemed real. The way he looked at her, keeping his gaze on hers, his eyes showing regret. Her heart pounded. Why did she have to read into things so much? He was probably just exhausted from his long day.

"I'll see you at seven," she whispered, fearful that her voice would give away her uneasiness. She wouldn't give him the satisfaction of knowing how he affected her as she raced to shut the door and hurry up the front stairs. With a shaking hand, she inserted the key and closed the door behind her. Her nerves were frayed.

It was only once she was inside that Doug had driven away. Just like he had always done—waited for her to be safe inside before driving off. Remembering those late night dinners and his patience with her erratic work schedules did something to her resolve to remain mad at him.

Sinking against the closed door, Paulina stared up at the ceiling. Now what to do with the very desirable Doug Brophy and her traitorous heart?

Chapter Four

Doug needed to collect his thoughts. Sitting at his desk nursing a steaming cup of black coffee, he studied the files on Peter Howlings and the reports on today's kidnapping. The room had cleared out since he had assigned available officers to other parts of the investigation and sent them into the field, but the TV still blared with the evening news. He had thought about calling it a day after he dropped off Paulina but, since his other officers were still working the case, it was only fair that he put in his time too. Not like he had a hell of a lot of time to solve it either.

A child's young voice caught his attention. "If Santa can't be found, we can't have Christmas," the little boy said into the microphone being held near his chin. Dressed in winter hat and mittens, his rosy cheeks shown brightly into the camera.

Doug swiveled in his chair for a better view of the screen.

"They said Santa Claus was taken today by bad guys. They need to bring him back. We want Christmas."

Behind him, a group of children and parents stood

huddled together just like they had been earlier at the mall.

"As you folks at home can see, children from across the area have converged in front of Melway Mall for a vigil for Santa's safe return. His kidnapping was witnessed earlier today by scores of second graders from a local elementary school here to sing Christmas carols. Word has spread like wild fire across the nation about Santa's ordeal today. Reports are steadily coming in from all states, and around the world, that panic has set in amongst young children who fear, that if Santa isn't found soon, Christmas this year is in jeopardy."

Lieutenant Caldwell stepped in front of the microphone. "I can assure all the children that everything is being done to get Santa back to the North Pole safe and sound so Mrs. Claus can take good care of him and have him ready for Christmas. All little boys and girls need to continue to be on their best behavior and listen to Mom and Dad because Santa will still know if you're naughty. As for particulars in the case, we won't discuss those due to the ongoing investigation and the sensitive nature of the case. We believe this to be an isolated case and that the public is not at risk. I promise any updates will be shared with the public immediately. That's all for now folks."

Lt. Caldwell stepped away from the crowd while the reporter spoke again. Doug smirked realizing the lieutenant stole his words from earlier. He made a mental note to bust his balls for showing his softer side.

"Stay tuned to this news channel for all news, sports and weather updates as well as the continued

Santa vigil growing by the minute at Melway Mall. Police do discourage any one from coming down here unless it's to shop. Considering the heavy retail congestion, police ask that vigils for Santa be done from the safety of homes where young children can stay warm."

"Holy shit, this is getting unreal," Doug said to the nearly empty room before turning back to his desk.

"Detective Brophy, do you want these?" Wanda from the mailroom asked holding a stack of envelopes.

"What are they?"

"Letters from kids asking for Santa's safe return. There's got to be about 500 here," she said, placing the piles wrapped in elastic bands on his desk.

"What? The kidnapping just happened this morning. There's no way mail could've come already."

"Now I didn't say anything about mail. These envelopes have been dropped off by teachers and parents. Seems the schools all had the children write letters on Santa's behalf as part of the grieving process after what they witnessed or heard." She shook her head and walked away. "The nerve of someone messing with Santa. You better catch the fools before the residents of this city do."

Doug was alone in the office with her departure, left to stare at the piles of odd shaped envelopes with scribbled handwriting on the outside.

"Great!" Now he had no choice but to solve the case for the childrens' sake. Screw the drug dealer. It was only about the children now.

His cell phone chimed and he searched his pocket for it. The caller ID listed the caller as unknown. He contemplated ignoring it and letting voice mail get it but maybe the bartender had come up with some valuable info.

"Brophy."

The terrified voice on the other end shot Doug to his feet. He'd recognize that voice anywhere, even masked by hysteria like it was now.

"Doug, I need help. They said things to tell you," Paulina said in a voice so shaky her words were barely audible.

Doug wasted no time and ran for his car, keeping the cell phone pressed to his ear. "Where are you? At home still?"

"Y-yes. He was really mad. Told... me... to... tell... you…" A loud sob cut off her words and pierced his chest with a sickening feeling. God help the person who scared her like this.

Doug spoke calmer than he felt, a powerful rage raced through his body like a tidal wave. "Paulina, honey, I'm on my way. You stay on the phone with me. I'm coming to you. I'll be there in minutes. Is the man who scared you still there?"

God he hoped so because the perp would be a fucking dead man as soon as he got his hands around the man's throat.

"N-no. Left after he said to tell you…back the fuck off." Her voice cracked, gone was the gentle, calm, soothing voice she always used at press conferences. Never once did he witness her crack under pressure and cursing was a rarity. Even today, she responded calmly to the childrens' tears and didn't allow the emotions swirling around her to interfere with her composure.

But now Doug could practically feel Paulina shaking. His hand gripped the steering wheel harder as his sirens blared and lights flashed while he sped thru evening traffic. *Come on! Come on! Move out of the fucking way, people!*

"Paulina, take a deep breath, honey. No one's going to bother you again. I give you my word." And he meant it. "I'm thirty seconds away. Stay on the line with me."

"O-ok." She inhaled and let out a long breath. "I'm sorry. I don't fall apart like this. It's just that…well, he was so mean. I didn't know what to do. I always know what to do, Doug."

He screeched to a halt in front of the house where he had dropped Paulina off not more than an hour ago. "Open your door and let me in, sweetheart." He ran up her stairs two at a time and bolted inside.

She jumped into his arms, her body still shaking, her cheek lay against his shirtfront as her nails dug into his chest. His arm wrapped around her as he shoved his cell into his coat pocket and kicked the door shut. The house looked in good order so it hadn't been ransacked. He gave her a few minutes to regain her composure, and once the trembling subsided, he pulled her away from him and studied her face.

Eyes swollen from crying, cheeks flushed, but the rest of her was very pale.

"Did he hurt you?"

She shook her head.

"Tell me everything, Paulina, don't leave any details out." His softly spoken words still came out as a command as he helped her to the sofa, sitting beside her, never taking his arm from around her.

Her small shoulders lifted then sagged like she carried heavy weights on them. "When you dropped me off, I showered. Just couldn't take another second of smelling like that bar."

Her slender hand swiped at the wetness on her cheeks. "Then I came down to the kitchen to fix dinner before I did some work. I heard a noise in the living room so I went to check it out. A man was standing there and said he had a gun but I didn't see it. He wore sunglasses and a hat. I couldn't see his face and didn't recognize him as anyone I knew."

She took a long breath and toyed with her fingers before she looked back up at him. "He walked up to me. I was frozen in place, couldn't move. He said to give the hotshot detective working with me a message. He said to tell you to back the fuck off or you won't like the consequences. When he trailed a finger down my arm, I thought…" She rubbed her arms up and down. "I freaked out. Shoved him. Christ, he didn't even budge. I shoved him again and he laughed at me. I tried to turn and run but he grabbed my wrists and dragged me up until I was practically dangling in the air." Her gaze never left his, her fear swirling within those watery depths of blue circles. "He told me that big trouble happened to little girls who interfered with the bad guys."

Doug was determined to find Santa if some skank thought he could terrorize an innocent woman. "I won't let anything happen to you, Paulina. That's a promise. We need to get you out of here, but staying at my place isn't a great idea since whoever visited you would surely be staking out my place too." He cradled her close to him, rubbing her arm and kissing the top of her head before he realized what he was doing.

32

A minute of silence ensued while he tried to think of a plan.

"My parents are away visiting my brother and his family before the holiday," her wavering voice said. "We can stay there. It's not far."

"Sounds like a plan. Get what you need and let's head out."

Doug checked all the doors and windows to secure her home before they drove to the house twenty minutes out of town. Paulina remained quiet in the front seat except a minimum of words to direct him to her parents' driveway.

Still ringing her hands in her lap, she glanced over at him. "I'm sorry I fell apart like that. I was just stunned to find someone standing in my house. I always lock my doors so I don't know how he got in."

"Through the cellar back door. I checked out the place while you threw your bag together and found that lock had been picked."

She gasped. "Oh, my God. Really?"

After parking in front of her parents' house, Doug opened the car door, grabbed her bag from the backseat, and followed her to the front door. "Whoever it was knew what he was doing."

"I thought the worst would happen. I really believed he was there to rape or kill me. I hadn't even thought about a connection to the investigation until he mentioned you."

Just the thought of someone violating her had Doug counting to ten mentally to keep from cursing out loud. "He was there to spook you. I'm so sorry he used you to get to me. You're off the case come tomorrow."

Paulina stepped inside and silenced the house alarm before facing him. "You're not taking me off this case, Doug. You don't tell the Mayor's Office what to do."

He stared at her. *Is she insane?*

"I do when their employee gets attacked because of me and the case I'm working. I'm sure the mayor will agree that your safety is more important than you babysitting me."

With her hands on her hips, she narrowed her eyes. "Is that what you think I'm up to? Babysitting you? Well, for your information, the mayor thought it'd give you more of a chance to perform your duties and resolve this case quickly if I were there to help with the intense media coverage by fielding their questions."

Crossing his arms, he dug in his heels. "Either way, I want you off the case."

"No."

He shook his head. Why did she have to pick now to be a stubborn woman? "No? Don't be foolish. Why would you want to put yourself in jeopardy?"

She stepped closer to him and angled her head up to glare at him, those gorgeous blue eyes still filled with fright. "Can I walk away, Doug? Huh? Can I? Don't you think I'm stuck in this either way? If you remove me, whoever attacked me will know they got to you. Then how safe will I be? Wouldn't I be safer with you than away from you? I mean, look what happened to me tonight after only being away from you for an hour."

Doug ground his jaw so hard it ached. Damn woman had to plead a decent argument, didn't she?

And she had to be right too! He ran a hand through his hair and turned away from her, but she moved in front of him again and pinned him with a steady challenge. "Fine, Paulina, you win. But only because I'd rather have you with me where I can protect you. But if you deliberately put yourself in harm's way or don't follow my directives, I swear I'll have you placed in protective custody until this case is finished. Understand?"

Her wide eyes roamed his face before she met his eyes again. "Agreed, Doug."

That was it? No argument? No rebuttal for his threat. Odd. He had expected her claws to come out with his demands.

"Thank you, Doug, for coming to my house so quickly. I'm really glad you're here with me." She rubbed his arm and stepped away to pick up her overnight bag.

Fiery goose bumps shot up his arm. His cock hardened and he resisted the urge to adjust his pants. What was it about this woman that one touch could have him ready to beg her for more? After all these months and their time apart, shouldn't the attraction have simmered down by now?

"Let me show you where you can sleep," Paulina said, walking toward the spiral staircase.

"I'll sleep down here on the couch where I can hear anyone trying to break in."

"Are you sure?" she asked, nervous eyes scanning the room.

Christ, he certainly couldn't sleep on the same floor as her. He hardly knew how he'd sleep in the same house without lying awake all night imagining her sexy body draped across soft sheets. "Yes," he managed without sounding desperate or edgy.

She disappeared upstairs and returned in a few minutes. "I'm starving. Gonna see what I can scrounge up in the kitchen that's quick and easy. You hungry?"

"Starved. If you take care of the food, I'll start a fire. We can eat by the fireplace to warm up," Doug replied, already moving to the hearth. Keeping busy would help keep his mind off her sexy body.

"Sounds like a plan," she said and disappeared from the room.

When Paulina strode back into the room holding two plates and two glasses on a carrying tray, Doug quickly jumped up to help her. They ate pizza by the fireplace as the flames filled the family room with a soft glow.

"Okay, I'm ready to hear your reason why, Doug," she said, placing her empty plate on the coffee table.

Sitting on the opposite end of the couch, he finished his last bite of pizza and wondered where he lost the conversation. "Reason for what?"

"For not calling me in June. For ignoring all my calls. For never returning my emails."

Shit, he should've expected this would come up while they were alone for the evening. Time to face the past. "I can't say I'm sorry enough, Paulina. I handled the whole situation badly. If it's any consolation, I never meant to hurt you."

"Yeah, well, you did. Now tell me why. Were you not attracted to me?"

Was she kidding? "Hell, no, that's not it. Why would you even think that?"

She shrugged. "Gee, I don't know. Guy takes you on a date a few times. Things get hot and heavy. Just when we're ready to jump into bed, poof, he's gone. Out of sight. Out of mind. Like I never existed. It hurt, Doug. It fucking hurt a lot. So forgive me for wanting a little more detail about why you needed to ignore me like I was the plague when you could've offered a simple explanation and allowed me to move on."

God, he wanted nothing more than to kiss those sexy lips and put that temper of hers to use in bed. But, she was right. He owed her a decent explanation. Now if only he could put it into words, without sounding like a total dick.

"In my defense, I had tried to call two months later. You refused the calls and never returned my messages."

"Yeah, well, by then I wasn't in the mood for your excuses and felt humiliated. My thoughts were a mess and I couldn't trust you not to break my heart all over again."

He owed her the truth after putting her through that. "You made me feel vulnerable, Paulina. Made me feel things I never had before and I wasn't quite sure how to handle those feelings. I looked forward to your calls, seeing you after work. Then I would kiss you and my mind would go blank for everything except you. If I closed my eyes, your amazing blue eyes and beautiful face were there. If I slept, your soft voice lulled me to sleep. If I touched you, I never wanted to let you go."

"Yet, that's exactly what you did. You let me go, Doug. When it was going pretty damn good." Her tone wasn't accusatory but sad. Her eyes reflected the pain she had shared with him moments ago and he felt like the scum of the earth.

"Believe me, Paulina, it's a decision I've regretted ever since. I've wanted to call you so many times to make things right."

"You should've talked to me instead of just ending it and leaving me hanging to wonder what I did wrong. The way you just explained things was the most romantic sentiment anyone has ever said to me." Her fist clutched her heart. "My, God. Don't you think I would've understood the need to take things slow and to get used to the new emotions? Don't you know I was falling for you too, Doug? Hard."

He dared to keep eye contact with her even though the impulse to pull her into his arms and kiss her until he got his fill overwhelmed him to the point of destroying all rational thoughts.

"If you ever thought of giving me a second chance, I'd like to pick up where we left off, Paulina. I swear there's been no other woman since you."

"And there's been no other man. But as much as I want to be with you again, I just need some time to forgive you. It's not because of the reasons you turned from me—it's the fact you did. When you're a couple, when you're with a partner, then it's got to be equal or it's never going to work out. You should've had enough faith in me, trusted me enough, to talk to me about how you felt. If we were to pick up and try again, I'd need to know you won't run when things move to the next level. I'd need to trust that you will be open with me."

"Understood. So will you let me know when I'm forgiven?" he asked, doing his damnedest to remain on his side of the couch and not seduce her until they were both naked and lying before the roaring flames in the hearth.

She slowly rose and stretched, the simple act of viewing her slender body causing his cock to grow even bigger than the erection that had started when they sat to eat. If ever he needed to proceed with caution, it was now. He couldn't fuck up the fragile truce they had just achieved.

"I promise, Doug, you'll be the first to know." The purr in her voice would've made his cock salute her if it was free from the constraints of his jeans.

Damn woman was driving him completely insane with lust. When she sashayed over to him, his heart thumped against his chest so loud he thought she might hear. What was she up to now?

Before he could wonder much more, she bent over him while he sat on the couch and lightly touched her lips to his. The brief hesitation before she pulled back had him sucking in air and staring at her light blue eyes shadowed with desire. "Good night, Doug. Pleasant dreams."

When she walked past him, he clenched his fists to keep from tugging her onto his lap for a real kiss. If she had stroked the outline of his cock in his jeans, he was sure he would've exploded in his pants. He turned to watch her walk to the stairs.

"I'm really glad you're here, Doug."

Her simple declaration comforted him more than he could explain. He was glad to be where he could keep her safe but, damn, what would keep his heart safe now that he might have another chance with her?

There was no doubt that she'd soon offer her

forgiveness, the look of serenity in her eyes and the smile on her lips spoke volumes. He'd pay the price for his lack of manners in June and wait for as long as Paulina deemed—until she could trust him again.

But she damn well better make up her mind soon or he'd die a slow death with wanting her.

Chapter Five

Paulina rubbed the chill from her arms even as her body heated. The ache between her legs hadn't subsided while she tossed and turned during the past hour. It was like her body sensed what was now so close. So she sought out the only cure for the throbbing emanating from deep within her.

Doug.

She crept down the spiral staircase, her bare feet cold against the hardwood floor. The heat was lowered only minimally during the night, but with winter's cold temps outside, there was no hope to keep the floor warm and she had forgotten her slippers in the haste to visit Doug where he slept before the fireplace.

What would his reaction be? He had made it clear that he wanted another chance. And it had been near impossible to banish him from her memories, no matter how hard she tried. Was she ready for rejection if that's what he offered? But what if he wanted her? Could she surrender her heart again?

Walking toward him, memories flooded her mind. All the hard work she had invested to get her career to a successful point. The long, sleepless nights of studying to be at the top of her class in college. The grueling hours of political campaigning for the man who eventually became her boss. The endless handshaking and smiling. Christ, she could have wrinkles just from that.

But even when people surrounded her, loneliness seemed to consume her. Going home to an empty house each night had been miserable, no one to greet her or share the events of her day. Being with Doug had given her someone she looked forward to seeing and she enjoyed the knowledge that he looked forward to seeing her.

Now inching closer to where Doug slept, Paulina remembered their time together before everything went wrong. His touch, his voice, his interest—all had given her an amazing feeling she hadn't experienced before him. Like he only had eyes for her. How many times had she lain awake at night wondering what she had done wrong to chase him away? Wondering how she could've done things differently with the first real relationship she had had since graduating college. It didn't matter now. Memories were just that—thoughts of the past. It was what faced her now that needed her complete attention.

Inside the stone hearth, a fading fire still glowed. Edging her way around the couch, she gasped when she didn't find him asleep on the couch. The blankets had been haphazardly brushed aside. Panic assailed her. Had the intruder from earlier followed them here? Was Doug in trouble?

She turned and slammed into a hard male chest.

A scream escaped her throat and she let her fists fly catching the man on the jaw. Her knuckles were in agony before the man could even groan. His jaw was made of stone. Didn't matter. This time she'd fight even harder.

A strong arm slid around her midsection and she battled like crazy to get away, wanting to scream for Doug but unable to form any more words with fear choking her.

"Christ, Paulina. It's me. Doug. Chill out."

She stopped struggling and squinted to see him in the darkened room. "Doug?"

He let go of her and walked to the fireplace. He quickly stoked the fire and the flames roared back to life, illuminating them in a fine glow, enough to now see each other's faces.

The first thing she noticed was how he rubbed his jaw as she massaged her sore hand. "Oh, my God. I punched you. Oh, Doug." She rushed to him. "I'm so sorry. I thought you were another intruder, and, well, what are you doing off of the couch?"

"What are *you* doing sneaking around the house?"

The heat from her cheeks definitely wasn't a result of the fire. How did she admit to coming down for a booty call without embarrassing herself to death? How did she tell him that he had made her too horny to sleep, and if he didn't fuck her soon, she'd lose her mind? How did she admit the past was the past and the future was worth fighting for?

"Does this mean I'm forgiven, Paulina?" he asked, his tone softer, his hands resting on her hips. The knowing look in his eyes reassured her motives.

"Yes."

"Okay, but first…no more sneaking around. I heard you creeping down the stairs and didn't know for sure if it was you so I got into position, just in case. No more sneaking, okay?"

She wrapped her arms around his neck. "No more ignoring me, okay?"

His smile widened from ear to ear. "Never again, sweetheart. You may get sick of me, but I promise to give you my complete attention."

A heaviness lifted off her shoulders. "I want you, Doug. I couldn't sleep. I just wanted to feel you against me…I want to pick up where we left off."

"Now those are the best words I've heard in a long time," he said, lifting her off her feet and placing her legs around his waist before sitting carefully on the couch. "Now where were we?"

His hand cupped the back of her head and pulled her down to him. Once his lips touched hers, the same incredible wave of pleasure, that she so fondly remembered, tore through her. But even with the familiarity of his kiss, there was something different. Before his kisses had been about intimacy, now they possessed, thrilled, consumed her. His tongue ran across the divide of her lips until they opened and let him enter. His mouth crushed against hers, his tongue battled hers for space. She moaned into his mouth, the sound swallowed but met with a groan of his own.

The crackling of the fire couldn't compete with their heavy breaths once they broke the connection to come up for air. With his lips sucking the side of her neck under her ear, Paulina expected to burst into flames with how hot he made her. It should be unlawful to kiss this good.

His hands pulled her flannel pajama top over her head, her breasts in plain sight for him to admire. By the way his mouth captured her nipple, she guessed he enjoyed them very much. Arching back from pure pleasure, she didn't worry about falling off his lap, not with his strong arm anchored around her waist. Feeling lively, she grabbed his head and pushed his mouth harder onto her flesh.

He obliged her with a scrape of teeth. Her cry echoed against the silence of the room.

Had she been crazy to work so hard on a career to forego this thrill? "Oh, Doug. I love it. Feels so good. More. I want so much more." Moaning the words, all thoughts of anything other than Doug's touch were driven from her mind.

His interest turned to her other nipple, sharing the same attention with a greedy mouth. Releasing her, he swung her onto her back to lie over his blankets on the couch.

"Oh, baby, you have no idea how much more I want. Our first time, I want to make it perfect for you," he said, breathless.

She tugged his shirt up his back and over his head. Her hands were busy sliding over taut muscles and heated flesh, the combination too sexy for her own good. Leaning up, she sank her teeth into the side of his neck, offering a little friskiness she had never felt before.

"Goddamn, Paulina, keep that up and I won't make it inside of you before I explode."

"Mmmm. I think I like you talking dirty…beats the hell out of being a gentleman."

His strangled voice reverberated throughout the room triggering a giggle to escape her. "Be careful, my dear. I admit I have very little control left. Teasing me with sexy words will put you on the fast track to being fucked until you forget your name. I want to have a little more finesse this first time."

She raked her nails over his shoulders, down his back as close as she could get to his ass. With her fingertips hovering at the top of his hard ass, she kneaded the tight skin earning more groans to her delight.

"Make me forget my name, Doug. I've waited so long for this."

"You and me both, honey."

His mouth claimed hers again as he performed some strange movements to wiggle both of them out of their pants. With her panties the last remaining barrier between their bodies, he went to work on clearing them away too. With a quick lift of his body off of hers, he peeled the thin cotton briefs from her and reached in his jean pocket for something.

He must've noticed her inquisitive stare because he answered her when she hadn't even asked a question. "Condom. Thank Christ I have some in my wallet."

She blew out a sigh of relief, knowing her body hummed too much to not feel him moving inside of her soon. She stretched her arm out and slid her fingers around his cock, stroking it, needing to feel the heaviness of it in her palm. The thick erection pulsed under her touch. His head swung back with a growl before his gaze returned to hers.

Paulina settled back on the couch to allow him to sheath his cock with the condom. The warmth from the fire heated the room nicely, but she preferred the warmth of Doug's body covering hers. It only took seconds for him to return, his strength apparent as he held his weight off of her and trailed light kisses down her belly to her inner thighs. Draping her legs over his shoulders, she cried out when he settled between her legs, his steaming breath teasing her pussy lips.

"Oh, Doug. Please. Just fuck me. You're…driving me…crazy." Even she couldn't recognize her own voice, masked in that husky sound filled with neediness.

"Just a taste, Paulina. I just want a taste of your sweetness." Without another word, Doug buried his face in her mound, his moist lips bathing her in wet kisses.

Her hands searched with crazed determination to grasp something, anything. Fisting her hands in the blankets was the best she could do with the limited space on the couch.

"Oh, this is wonderful. Don't…stop."

"Mmmm. Not until you come for me," he said, the words falling against her swollen lips. His large hands caressed her legs keeping them in place over his shoulders.

She melted into the couch. Unable to take a deep breath or fight the impending pleasure any more, she succumbed to his manipulations and rode out the orgasm that roared through her.

"Yes! Yes! Oh. Yes!" Single sounds were all she could manage.

But Doug allowed her no time to recover from the sensations riveting her body. He climbed over her, burying his cock deep inside her with one long thrust.

"Paulina! Christ. Feels so good. Oh, God, baby. Too good."

He held still inside her for only a few seconds before cursing under his breath and continuing his pumping action. "I can't stop myself, Paulina. I'm ready to come already. Want…to…feel you…come too."

Again? Was he insane? She couldn't handle the pressures deep within her womb, like a thousand fiery fingers caressed every intimate muscle within her. But her pleasure was at his mercy. With each thrust, he edged her closer and closer to yet another explosive orgasm. Never had she had two orgasms so close together. How would she handle it when her legs shook and her pussy throbbed like a fast drumbeat?

"Doug, faster. Faster." Her limp body fought to gather strength, worried that the pressure building within her womb would overwhelm her.

When he leaned further onto her and buried his face into her hair, she was pleased to bathe her senses in the hot male flesh and the musky scents swirling around her. Heat rose from their bodies. Breathing deepened. Inaudible words sounded. And a memory was born.

Doug stiffened, his cock buried deep inside her, his arms trembling with the attempt to hold most of his weight off her, but she clung to his shoulders not wanting to lose the connection. Her orgasm matched his. With each thrust, he held inside her signaling his explosion, she cried out and rode the powerful spasms within her pussy. They were stronger than the first time, throbbing so much she wanted to clamp her legs together. She didn't know how to survive such pleasure.

"Doug!"

Soft kisses covered her jaw as her arms fell to her side and Doug lifted himself. Her arms were useless to hold him, feeling more like spaghetti than limbs.

"You're so friggin' beautiful, Paulina," he whispered, his face inches from hers. The fire must've died down some because it was hard to see his eyes but there was just enough light to see the dreamy twinkle within the brown depths. She did that to him. *Hey, how about that?*

Doug stepped away long enough to dispose of the condom and caught her around the waist when she crawled off of the couch.

"And where does this fine lady think she's going?"

"To bed. You exhausted me." As if on cue, she yawned unable to fight the amazing contentment settling deep into her bones.

"Okay," Doug said, pulling her with him onto the couch and covering both of them with the blanket.

On the table, she noticed his gun and reality came crashing back. Someone had tried to scare both of them off this case. And Santa was still missing. Children everywhere slept tonight wondering if there'd be a Christmas.

"Doug?"

"Mmmm," he offered, his soft breaths proving he had regained his composure and sleep was tempting him too.

"Do you think Christmas can be saved this year? I mean, we don't have a lot of time. Just under a week before the big day."

"Of course. We don't really have a choice."

She lifted her head from his chest and looked up

into his eyes. They were barely open. "How do you mean?"

He tried to shrug. "Kids are counting on us. So there's no choice. We need to make sure they all get their Christmas."

Without realizing it, she teared up. "How come you never showed this big heart of yours to me before?"

He smirked, eyes closed. "Because you never got me naked before."

She laughed, the sound coming all the way from her toes. "There'll be plenty more times of that."

"I like how you think, Paulina," he said, kissing her head and squeezing his arm around her tighter.

Yeah, she could sleep easy tonight, and not just because she lay in the arms of the man she had missed for six long months. But because she really believed he would find Santa...for the childrens' sake.

Chapter Six

Paulina sipped her second cup of coffee, not really needing the caffeine lift today. After waking in Doug's arms following a night of fantastic sex, she didn't need any artificial stimulants. Her high came from an all-natural satisfaction. Making a pledge to take more time for herself, and let her career flourish on its own, had been liberating.

"Now this is interesting," she said, perusing one of a dozen criminal files she and Doug had poured over since arriving at his office an hour ago.

"What is?" Doug asked from across the desk.

She glanced up and admired how sexy he looked with a shoulder harness, carrying a mean looking gun, strapped over his tight T-shirt. His sandy brown hair wasn't as tousled today as it had been last night in the heat of passion.

Not the time to think of that, though. Not in the middle of a police precinct surrounded by Doug's coworkers.

"This police log recorded an arrest for Peter Howlings four months ago, about one month before the drug raid where he fled on foot and avoided capture."

Doug shrugged. "Doesn't surprise me, Paulina. You'll find that a lot of these creeps are repeat offenders. They're either too stupid to learn a lesson the first time they're arrested or they're part of a vicious circle of family crime. Sadly, most know no other life than one of crime."

"No, I don't mean that. The police log has a notation of the arrest, but there's no notation in his criminal file of that particular arrest."

That caught Doug's interest as he came around the desk and peered over her shoulder, flipping through pages and studying reports.

"The arresting officer is Jim Bowler," Doug said. "I know he's had some disciplinary action with Internal Affairs."

"But why would he arrest someone and there not be a report, only one line on a police log?" she asked totally confused. Something wasn't right here.

"Because whatever the suspect had interested Bowler more than locking up a criminal." Doug's tone didn't hide his disgust.

Paulina read the police log. "It says here an arrest made for unknown drugs."

Doug tapped a finger on the file. "That's because Bowler conveniently failed to do a report, took the drugs for himself and thought no one would ever discover his plan because we're a smaller town."

"It also says Howlings was stopped on Eastern Avenue. That's in the vicinity of the bar we visited, *Charlie's Rack 'em and Sack 'em*. Oh, my God, Doug." She looked up at him. "Do you think Bowler could be the fancy dressed guy who hung out with Howlings at the bar?"

Doug stole a sneaky, quick kiss before speaking. "I'd bet any amount of money on it. Come on."

"Where are we going?" she asked as he tugged on her hand, pulling her up to stand beside him.

"Going to visit that friendly bartender again. But this time, we'll be armed with a picture and see if good old bartender dude IDs Bowler."

"And if he does?" she asked, putting on her coat while he pulled on his.

"Then we're that much closer to finding the missing Santa."

Walking past the front desk as they left the precinct, more news coverage on Santa's kidnapping caught their attention.

Paulina stopped and stared at the TV. "Oh, wow. It's on national news stations now. Look, it says will there be a Christmas? Oh, my God. Why are they allowing this to hype up? Don't they realize little kids are going to be heart broken? And for what? Ratings?"

"It could be worse. They could be broadcasting that Santa doesn't exist and ruining thousands of childhoods." Doug took her by the elbow and began walking outside again. "We've got the best lead yet. Let's hope we can resolve this case by the end of the day."

"That'd be very nice," she said, settling into the front seat of his car.

"It will be. I want another night like last night," he said, winking before turning into traffic. "I just wish we were in private now because I am dying to kiss you."

When he lifted her hand and kissed her knuckles, the simple romantic gesture thrilled her. "Let's get this case over with then we'll have all the time in the world for kissing."

****

The bartender proved a bit more cooperative than the other day. "Look, yeah, that's the guy. That's The Player. He's known as the supplier. Never sells the shit directly. Has goons who will do it for him."

Doug slammed his fist on the bar. "Stop fucking with me. Spill what you know or I'm putting word on the street that you're a rat bastard and outed every criminal who comes into this place."

The bartender swore and shook his head. "I heard he's a fucking cop, okay? He takes the stash from drug dealers he pulls over and gives it to the guys who hang with him and they sell it. But he's pissing off the other gangs in the drug trade something bad by creeping on their territory, especially when it's their guys who are getting their shit confiscated and sold by a cop."

"You should've been straight with me yesterday. I oughta run you in right now for interfering with a police investigation."

The bartender lit a cigarette. "Don't blow smoke up my ass, dude. We both know you have bigger fish to fry than me. Now stop fucking coming around here. Place starts crawling with cops and my customers won't come in. I've given you all I know. Can I have some peace now?"

"You've been more than helpful. Better look into cleaning this place up," Doug said, pushing the picture of Bowler back into his pocket before holding Paulina's hand and walking out of the bar.

"Now what, Doug? This is huge. We have a crooked cop loose on the streets of Shelby. Do you think he had something to do with Howlings' kidnapping?" Paulina asked, hugging her jacket shut against the cold.

"Hell, yeah. But why? I haven't figured that part out."

"Maybe Howlings threatened to turn him in or something," Paulina offered.

Doug opened her door before walking around to his. With the heat blaring, the car warmed up quickly. "I need to go see my lieutenant immediately. Let him know of my suspicions. Given that it's about an officer under his authority, this won't go over well. I really hope it's not true."

"I think that's the best plan. You need more help than me now. Can you drop me at my office while you do that? I need to check emails and get some work done," Paulina said, sure her voicemail was full since she hadn't had a moment to check it since last night. Something she had never done before.

Doug shot her a hostile glance. "No. You're not getting out of my sight until this is resolved. Now with a crooked cop, everything just got a lot more intense and dangerous."

"Doug. I work in city hall and there's a police officer assigned to the Mayor's Office. I'll be fine. If it will make you feel better, I'll even promise to stay inside until you can pick me up."

He drove calmly in the late morning traffic. "I don't like the idea," he said, keeping his eyes on the road. "This whole fucking Santa shit is messed up. Why would Howlings even take a job as a Santa if he was making money selling drugs for Bowler?"

"Maybe he was using the Santa gig as a front to sell drugs?" Paulina thought everything over for a minute. Then another idea dawned on her. "Blackmail. Maybe Bowler was blackmailing Howlings with that arrest. Howlings would've thought he'd be arrested or framed and would've done what any cop wanted."

Doug glanced at her when they stopped at a traffic light. "You are way too smart for the Mayor's Office, sweetheart. In fact, you should be the mayor. With your brains running the show, Shelby would be the best town in the country."

"It already is. Because you're here," she said when he stopped in front of city hall, the old brick building decorated with lights for the holiday. Busy shoppers hustled by carrying shopping bags and bracing against the cold winds.

"I'll walk you up," Doug said, turning off the ignition.

"No. I'm a big girl. Just watch me from the sidewalk. Then you need to get to the lieutenant and, with any luck, we'll have Santa saved. Plus, you'll get a drug dealer and the crooked cop in jail by tonight." She smiled. "And then you're mine."

A smile lit up his face. He was so friggin' handsome with his day old beard and prowling eyes. Her heart skipped a beat.

"Okay. You stay put here 'til I get back. I'll come to your office when I'm done."

"Yes, Detective Brophy." She shut the door after blowing him a kiss and walked into the building, saying hello to scores of fellow employees as she rushed to her office.

The elevator was empty for a change when she

slipped on, pressed the button for her floor and hit the button to close the door. But, as it happened hundreds of times before, a hand slipped between the closing doors, forcing them to open again. Damn! Why can't people learn to wait for the next elevator? Being polite, Paulina stepped aside to allow the next person in. She lazily checked her watch and looked up.

She gasped as the doors shut behind the man facing her, evil eyes narrowed on her.

Officer Jim Bowler.

Chapter Seven

Doug answered his cell phone on the way to the office. The caller ID displayed a generic phone number for the precinct. "Brophy."

"Marlin here. Your kidnapped Santa just wandered into a clinic downtown looking for medical assistance. He's said to be pretty banged up. Got the shit kicked out of him from what the doctor on site says. She wants to call an ambulance and transport him to the hospital but, considering the press coverage, she thought it best to contact us for advice. She doesn't want her practice overrun with media."

"Tell her not to call an ambulance until I get there. I'll be there in five minutes."

Doug disconnected and turned in the direction of the clinic with lights and sirens. How in the hell did the missing Santa escape his captors?

Doug didn't know if he'd get many answers.

One look at Peter Howlings and it was apparent someone beat the crap out of him since he'd been abducted. Following the ambulance, Doug escorted the victim, suspect, whatever he was, into the Emergency Room, flashed his badge at the triage nurse, quietly explaining the situation, and was shown immediately into a room with only the necessary medical staff knowing the true identity of the patient.

Santa Claus.

"Remember, all of his clothes are to be bagged for evidence, please," Doug said to the nurses cutting the bloodied Santa suit from Howlings.

Doug stepped up to the side of the bed as the nurse took his vitals. "Peter Howlings? I'm Detective Brophy, Shelby Police. I'm investigating your abduction yesterday. Mind answering a few questions so we can get the perps who did this to you?"

"It was a misunderstanding. I'm not pressing charges."

Doug let out a long breath. "Kidnapping's against the law. Not really up to you to press charges when the government can."

"Then it was only a stunt. You know. For publicity."

Doug crossed his arms and studied the battered man. "Then I hope to hell you're ready to reimburse the town of Shelby for a whole lotta police overtime. While you played a publicity stunt, we were busting our asses trying to find you. That's gonna be hundreds of thousands of dollars." Doug knew he was stretching the truth a bit but he wanted to make a point.

"I don't know anything," Howlings said through a badly split lip.

"Well, either way you'll be headed to prison for a really long time. Either for staging a fake kidnapping, which from the looks of you, someone forgot to *pretend* fight. Or for endangering the public safety with a publicity stunt, which again looks like it got way out of line. Or why don't we forget all those petty charges and go for the big one. Drug dealing charges. With your record, that's bound to get you life in prison. No more chances left for you now, Howlings."

Howlings turned and screamed, "What the fuck do you want from me?"

Doug leaned closer, keeping his voice stern but low. "I want your fucking cooperation, asshole. Thanks to you, dressing up like Santa Claus, all the little kids in the world think Christmas is ruined. What in the hell are you doing working as Santa anyway? Not pulling in enough cash with the drug sales, Howlings?"

"Fuck!" Howlings yelled. "I wanna leave."

Doug slapped a handcuff on Howlings' wrist and attached the other end to the stretcher when the man tried to pull himself into a sitting position. "You ain't going anywhere. Remember, you're butt naked, pal."

"What are you doing?" Howlings asked, jingling the cuff against the metal bar.

"You're under arrest," Doug replied.

"For what? I'm the fucking victim."

"We'll see about that." Doug's cell phone rang. He noticed Paulina's number and cheered up instantly. "Shut up, Howlings. I need to take this." Doug stepped outside the room but stayed on watch. "Hey, babe. You'll never believe what happened."

"Oh, I'd like to make a guess," a man's voice said with calm fury.

Doug felt the blood drain from his face. "Bowler." He cursed silently. "What have you done with Paulina?"

A malicious laugh echoed over the line and Doug

swallowed hard. "Nothing yet. But…now…that all depends on you. Are you a stupid cop, Brophy? Or a smart one?"

"What do you want?" Doug was cornered. Without knowing how or where Paulina was, he'd never be able to protect her like he promised.

"It's simple. An even exchange. Santa for this pretty little lady. He has my money and I have your girl. Now let's trade."

"How do I know you have her?"

Shuffling could be heard from the other end. "Doug." Paulina's voice. Then silence.

Fuck! Fuck! Fuck!

Doug was about to attempt the bluff of a lifetime. God help Paulina if he couldn't pull it off. "Listen, Bowler. I have a bag of money here. There's a lot and you can have it all. I don't give a shit about it. Found it stashed in his suit. No one knows about it but me. In fact, I'm the only cop here so far. So let's get this done before the fucking Calvary arrives. The money's not even tagged and, as far as I'm concerned, there was no money with him when he arrived here no matter what he claims. It'll be my word against his and you know they'll believe me."

"All I want is my money. Then I'm taking an early retirement and disappearing. I'll be damned if I go to jail because that fuckhead tried to rip me off and riled my temper."

"I don't give a fuck what you do," Doug said. "Just let me have the girl and you take the money and split."

"Show up at my favorite bar in one hour. You know the one where you've been asking questions about me. Bring the money. Take the girl. We both walk away with what we want. Try to fuck me over and I'll put a bullet through her pretty little head. No cops. Just you. You don't arrive solo then she'll never have a chance. Hope I make myself clear."

"Crystal clear. One hour I'll be there. And, Bowler, don't let my willingness to comply with your demands fool you. Touch one fucking hair on her head and I'll make you wish *you* were dead."

Bowler's laugh echoed across the line before the call disconnected.

"Nurse, get security up here quickly, but quietly," Doug ordered.

Doug dialed his cell. "Hey, bro, no time to talk. I'm going to need you to watch my back. Can you meet me in thirty? And pull your team together. Whoever you can get. Life and death, bro. I need you."

Doug got the answer he expected and gave his brother a meeting location. Once he briefed security on his prisoner in the trauma room, he'd be on his way to the most important meeting of his life.

He was stupid enough to walk away from Paulina once because he had feared falling in love with her. Now that the ache in the middle of his chest confirmed that love, he was damn sure not going to lose her for a second time.

Chapter Eight

Garrison stood taller and wider than Doug, but Doug's big brother wasn't half as pissed as he was right now. Doug's fists had been clenched since stepping out of his car and into the park that provided some cover with its foliage. They needed privacy to discuss their plans.

"Man, you really love this girl, huh, little bro?" Garrison asked, surrounded by three of his former Special Ops teammates. There wasn't anyone else Doug could think of to better protect his back and help rescue Paulina than the four men staring back at him, dressed in military fatigues, arms crossed, patience etched on their face amongst a host of scars. Each man stood proud and ready.

Exactly what Doug needed.

He stooped down and drew a sketch in the dirt using a branch. "Here's the bar, there's usually a group over here playing pool. Main room is here and I didn't see another exit but there's bound to be one. It's not a huge place so either he's holding her in a back room or the basement. Place is dark, typical shithole."

"Listen up," Garrison said in his no-nonsense

way. "Buck and Jack, take the side. When we enter, you'll go straight here." He made an X to indicate the spot on the ground. "Me, Shark, and Doug will head straight for the bartender and have him take us to where Bowler is hiding the girl."

"I want her alive so no blowing shit up in there, bro," Doug said, needing to feel some kind of control in this madness.

"Aw, hell, man. I told them they'd get to explode things." The other men smirked. "Ok. Back to the plan. It don't get any simpler than this, boys. In. Out. Don't repeat. No mistakes. Get the hostage. Fuck up anyone who stands in the way. If we have to shoot to kill, well, then there's one less scumbag on the street."

"Shooting's the last thing I want. I don't want Paulina hurt."

"Then let us do what you asked us to come here to do with you, little brother. We've got your back and hers. Everyone ready?"

The group grunted and piled into Garrison's truck after outfitting themselves in earpieces, shoulder harnesses, and weapons.

The drive to the bar was a quick one but every second Paulina spent alone with Bowler was one too long. Doug felt trapped within the truck, suffocating. He just wanted to be there with her.

Garrison wasted no time once in the parking lot. He parked directly across from the front of the entrance and hollered, "Move out."

Without a word, the group exited the vehicle, weapons drawn, and entered the establishment. As discussed, they moved to where they were assigned, spreading out evenly with precise movements.

The bartender had no time to react. "What the fuck?" he yelled, before Doug jumped the bar and grabbed him by the throat. Garrison and Shark surveyed the room, ready to pounce should someone interfere.

"Where's Bowler holding the girl?"

The bartender nodded to the left indicating a closed door.

"See my friends over there?" Doug asked and the bartender nodded. "Interfere in any way and they'll fuck you up so you'll drink through a straw for the rest of your life. Understood?"

The bartender nodded and Doug threw him aside, moving to the office door with Garrison and Shark taking stand on both sides.

Doug knocked three times, loud. "Bowler. Brophy. Open up. Got the cash."

The doorknob turned and the door cracked open. Doug stepped inside, not shutting the door. Paulina stood next to Bowler with a gun pointed at her head and tears in her eyes. Her hands were crudely taped in front of her with duct tape, another piece across her mouth. Other than a bruised cheek, she appeared in good shape.

"Open the bag," Bowler demanded.

Doug obliged. "Don't worry. It's all there. Told you I don't want the money. Just the girl."

Bowler's grin promised evil. "Maybe I don't want to give the girl up after all. I've kind of grown fond of her these past few hours. She's very pretty."

He saw red and pictured choking the life out of him. "Bowler, I did what you said. Here's your fucking money," Doug said between clenched teeth and whipped the bag at Bowler who didn't even flinch, allowing the bag to fall at his feet. If only he had made a grab for the money, Doug would've had the chance, with the gun away from Paulina's temple, to tackle him. *Fuck!*

"Hmmm. Seems now I've got the money and the girl," Bowler said.

From behind him, with not even a sound to warn Doug that they had entered the room, Garrison spoke. "I'd think twice about harming the girl, asshole. Doug here would have to shoot you. And if he didn't, then I would. Oh, please give me a reason to shoot your sorry ass."

"Who the fuck are you?" Bowler's eyes narrowed and he pinned his gaze on Doug, his fingers tightening around the gun. "Thought I said no fucking cops?"

"You did," Doug said calmer than he felt. "That's why I brought my brother and his friends along. Special Ops. Paulina, walk over here please."

Bowler shook her arm and she made a sound caught by the tape at her mouth. Three guns leveled at Bowler's head, the standoff too intense.

"The girl. Keep your fucking money. Give me the girl. That's all I came for and we leave. Then you get to split," Doug said using every ounce of control he could muster to keep from putting a bullet between Bowler's eyes.

"Yeah, right. Do you really take me for a fool? I give you the girl and you have me. No fucking way. I walk out of here with the girl and, when I get in my truck, she can go."

"Just let me shoot him, Doug," Garrison said like he was bored.

Doug concentrated on Bowler. "Look, I'm not about to blow my career because I gave you drug money for my girl's release. So as much as I'd love to see you behind bars, I'll pass this time. Come on, Paulina, we're leaving. And these guys come with me, Bowler. Your only other choice is getting shot. Give me the girl."

Beads of sweat collected on Bowler's forehead. "Fine. But try anything, and at least one of you will die along with me."

Paulina walked toward Doug. He grabbed her arms and whisked her from the room.

Garrison and Shark backed out slowly when Doug glanced back over his shoulder, his arm secured around Paulina's waist. He whistled for Buck and Jack to know the hostage was rescued and rushed to the entrance. Once outside, he half dragged Paulina around the truck for shelter. Using a pocketknife, he sliced away at the duct tape on her wrists then slowly peeled away the tape over her mouth.

"Did he hurt you in any way?" His fingers touched the small bruise on her cheek.

"No. Just a slap when I tried to resist him throwing me in his truck." She collapsed against him, her arms circling his back. "Doug, I thought I was dead. As soon as I got into the elevator, he was there. I couldn't do anything to save myself because I thought he'd shoot innocent people if I yelled."

"Bastard's lucky I didn't kill him."

Garrison and Shark remained by the entrance with Buck and Jack still inside.

"Why didn't you arrest him? You're going to let him get away?" she asked, looking up at him, her face pale and horrified.

"Ahh, my dear. Garrison and his guys will take care of him while I call my lieutenant."

After a briefing to Lt. Caldwell, Doug hung up. "Back up's on the way," he told Paulina, holding her by his side, keeping an eye on Garrison. "While you were being held hostage, Santa escaped his captors and now is in the hospital. My lieutenant is preparing a press conference so all the little boys and girls can sleep well tonight. Santa will be okay."

"Bowler admitted kidnapping Santa because he stole his money from drug deals. Howlings hid out as Santa to live in disguise. Dumb move for all of them," Paulina said, her exhaustion evident in her eyes. "Thank God this ordeal is over."

"Get down," Doug commanded, drawing his gun after pushing Paulina to the ground. "Bowler just walked outside," Doug gave a play-by-play account. "And as expected, Buck and Jack have him in custody. Sorry. Here, let me help you up."

Offering her his hand, Doug hauled her to her feet and into a hug. His lips caught hers. Tasting her warmth again was pure heaven. Relief flooded his veins, knowing how close he came to losing her forever. Breaking the kiss, he stared into her eyes. "Don't know what I would've done if I lost you. Next time, I walk you inside."

She laughed, sweet music to his ears. "I'll never turn that offer down again," she said, her voice no longer shaky.

****

Sirens blared and grew closer. Within seconds, the parking lot had filled with police cars and media vans.

Lt. Caldwell found Doug and offered his hand. "Good job, Brophy. Ms. Smithfield, are you all right?"

"Yes. Doug rescued me." She never wanted to let go of the man who risked his life to save hers. She loved him. She couldn't deny her heart any more. From the love that started six months ago, bloomed awareness that Doug was meant to be with her. From the way he held her, she hoped he felt the same way.

"Good, then let's get this press conference over. This town's been in the national spotlight for two days now and I don't like it one bit," Lt. Caldwell complained. "Would love some peace and quiet."

Lt. Caldwell stepped in front of the reporters, each awaiting information. "Members of the media, I'm Lt. Caldwell of the Shelby Police Department. I'm pleased to report that after delicate and intense police work by the Shelby Police Department, Santa has been found safe and sound after being kidnapped from Melway Mall yesterday morning. He's currently being examined by medical staff at a local hospital and is expected to receive a good bill of health in order to be ready for Christmas Eve. So to all the boys and girls who have kept such a long vigil for Santa, I want to thank them for their courage to believe in the good things in life. Each child in Shelby, and across the nation, rallied by Santa's side when he needed them most, offering prayers and wishes for a safe return. Now, we have just that. Good night."

"May we speak with the detective responsible for saving Christmas?" a reporter asked.

Lt. Caldwell smiled. "Of course. Detective Brophy's persistence with this case and his exceptional skills as one of our valued detectives were vital to a positive outcome. Detective Brophy, will you answer a few questions?"

Doug stepped in front of the group of reporters holding microphones and notepads. He never let go of Paulina's hand and the simple touched warmed her to her toes.

"Detective Brophy, how does it feel to be credited with saving Christmas?" a woman asked from the pack.

Doug smiled and glanced down at Paulina, his eyes twinkling in the flickering cameras. "I'm very pleased with the outcome of the case, but I'm afraid Christmas saved me instead. It got me back the woman I let slip away."

The crowd sighed. Paulina just wanted to curl up with Doug on the couch and never leave his arms.

"Detective Brophy, what are your plans for the future now that this big case is behind you?"

"Now that depends on if Paulina says yes," Doug said, peeking at her with a wide smile.

"Says yes? What's the question?" another reporter asked as Paulina stared at Doug wondering if she was hearing him right.

Doug turned to Paulina, his arms resting on her waist. "Will she give me a second chance so we can see how many Christmases we can spend together?"

After many gasps, the crowd quieted down. All Paulina could do was stare at Doug.

"How about it Paulina? You willing to stay in this relationship with me for the long run?"

Emotions of every sort—happiness, nervousness, excitement—swirled through her, jumbling her thoughts to the point she fought to form words. But all she needed was one.

"Yes," she said, jumping into his arms and laying her lips against his.

The crowd around them erupted in cheers and claps then began caroling.

It didn't matter how cold the weather was now that the winter season was in full blast. The heat from Doug kept Paulina warm in his embrace, just like she knew the love in both their hearts would keep them happy for the Christmases to come.

Breaking the kiss, she touched his cheek. "I love you, Doug. So much."

His hand covered hers, turned it over and kissed the palm. "Love you, too, Paulina. Always."

For the Love of a WOMAN

Christina James

Chapter One

Mitch drifted off to sleep, warring with the visions behind his eyelids when the dream took hold.

Transported back to that horrible day, terror gripped him by the throat, defying his attempts to suck in air with desperate breaths. Fear's icy fingers crawled along his sweat-dampened skin like a slimy worm slithering across a rain-slicked ground. But Mitch couldn't let fear win. If he did, death would surely follow. He could only fight his way out of the nightmare.

Moving quietly along the liquor store's dark hallway to the backroom where the girls were held captive, Mitch relied totally on his specialized police training to guide him to the hostages. His eyes scanned the darkness, adjusting to the lack of light. His ears strained for any sound but found only silence. The ominous scent of death—the smell of spilled blood—made his heart pound painfully within his chest.

Mitch's mind filtered a thousand vicious curses as he inched forward, desperate to reach the girls who depended on him for their lives.

Time passed too slowly as he ignored his own

pain and crept onward into the darkness, maybe to his death.

His gun steady in his hand, his senses on high alert. The second he viewed the figure lying on the ground, motionless in a dark pool of liquid, his world changed forever. And not for the better.

Mitch woke abruptly in a cold sweat, his skin chilled and clammy. The way his heart pounded, he felt like he had just run a marathon. He pinched the bridge of his nose and shook the sleep from his foggy mind. Sitting behind the steering wheel in his truck while using the seat's headrest as a pillow only cramped his muscles. Taking a nap on the side of the road wasn't conducive to a decent rest. A quick glance at the clock showed he'd been asleep for just under an hour. And he felt worse now than when he pulled over to rest his bleary eyes.

Turning the ignition, the engine roared to life and Mitch pulled his truck back onto the rural highway. He was tired, hungry, and lost somewhere in the damn Smoky Mountains. Running from a past that haunted him to a future he couldn't see would have been better with a direction in mind. Small drops of water splattered on his windshield, just a hint of the storm brewing in the east.

He had driven with no particular destination. But for the first ten hours on the road, he had an idea of where the hell he was. Not now. Now, huge green fields dotted with grazing cows and horses seemed never ending. Deep forests with tall, leafy trees and ragged undergrowth abutted the fields. And still there was no sign of civilization. The two-lane backcountry route was an infinite winding road. Like being stuck in a maze with no way out. Similar to what his memories did to him, keeping him stuck in the past, stuck on one day with no way out.

The once deep blue skies held dark gray puffy clouds and threatened rain. His six-foot-two inch frame ached from being cramped behind the wheel for so many hours. His fault really for driving with no purpose. A glance in the rearview mirror confirmed that he looked as bad as he felt. His eyes were bloodshot, the tiny red lines making the whiskey color of his eyes dark and menacing. Gray half-moons had set in under his eyes, causing him to look old and withered. Scratchy dark stubble covered an angular jaw that gave his chin an angle of defiance, jutting out just enough to square his face. His thick, light brown hair cried out for a haircut.

The "ding ding" alarm sounded just as big fat raindrops hit the windshield. The tiny picture of a red gasoline pump on his dashboard warned of low fuel. He burst out laughing, laughing so hard that it hurt. It was either laugh or punch the windshield and that would just let in the heavy rain now lashing out from mean skies.

Ding, ding.

"All right, for Christ's sakes. I'll get you some go-go juice as soon as I find some sign of life around here," he complained, while straining his head to look into the distance through the rain-spotted windshield.

Slowly, Mitch drove through the downpour. Scanning the distance, there was no sign of people anywhere. The mountains were a huge mass of land and he cursed himself for not paying attention to his whereabouts.

His arms tensed, holding the steering wheel, while his thoughts wandered to the recent events that had left him in this current predicament. He still couldn't believe that he had really left his home, his life, his job. Everything. Just ran. There was nothing left for him now in Boston. Only haunting memories and a job with the police force that was out of reach. His conscience weighed heavier and heavier each day. He only hoped the distance from Massachusetts would help ease the pain. Wherever the steering wheel turned, he'd go but not for long without some gas and sleep.

There might be enough gas for another few miles…maybe. He smirked when he saw the old green and white sign on the side of the road indicating the Town of Courtsville two miles ahead. With the rain pelting the windshield, he sure was glad to find civilization again.

Lightening streaked across the sky, spotlighting the distant mountains. Thunder crackled with deafening roars. The wind shook his truck, blowing through the trees and slanting them toward the roadway. No way in hell did he want to get stranded in a friggin' thunderstorm with no food or water and no damn aspirin. He didn't know what hurt more, the pain between his eyes or his knee.

"Just like in the movies," Mitch complained, squinting to see through the stream of water pouring over the windshield. Small hailstones bounced off the glass like ping pong balls. On the roof, it sounded like drums.

He slowed, squinted, and almost drove right by the one-island gas station. There were no lights on. No sign of anyone working. What the fuck? To his relief, when he pulled up to the pump, he glimpsed a dim light in the window of the small shack. The front door opened as a tall, white-haired elderly man in overalls holding an umbrella stepped out.

Mitch rolled down his window. "Fill 'er up, please," he directed, unfastening his seatbelt to get his wallet.

"You ain't from around here, are ya?"

"No, sir." Mitch caught bright blue eyes watching him. He wasn't looking for conversation. Just some fuel.

The man started to pump the gas. Mitch was rolling up his window when the guy reappeared.

Mitch stared at him in bafflement. "What?"

"Can't very well talk to the hose while she fills ya up, so thought I'd talk to you."

"About what?"

"Don't know."

Small towns. Is this what people did? Make idle conversation just to hear themselves? "Well, I don't have much to talk about. Been on the road too long." As proof, he yawned, unable to stop himself.

"You got far to go?" the man asked, holding the umbrella as the rain slowed to a light drizzle. Thunder still echoed in the distance. At least the storm had passed.

"Not sure. But I could use dinner and a night's sleep. Can you tell me if I'm anywhere near either?"

"Not gonna get far in this truck," the man announced, angling his head toward the hood. "Nope. Not more than two miles I'd say."

Now he had Mitch's attention. "Why?" Mitch

79

followed the man's glance. A large plume of white smoke bellowed from under the hood. "Son of a bitch!"

Before Mitch finished another line of curses and managed to get out of the truck, the old man was already standing in front of the hood.

"Pop it," the man commanded.

Mitch complied, reaching under the steering column and pulling the black lever until he heard a pop. He walked slowly to stand by the old man who used his hand to brush away the smoke.

"Yup. Just as I thought. You cracked the radiator. Ain't no antifreeze or water left in 'er." He shut the hood. "It'll get you about two miles but not more without stalling or worse, blowing the engine."

"Shit!" Mitch stood with his hands on his hips and studied the shack. There was no sign of a garage, but he had to ask. "Can you fix it?"

"Wish I could help you there, my friend, but I only sell gas. There's a good mechanic in town."

"Can I get to him without causing more damage?"

"Sure, I guess. But won't do you any good. He's closed up shop by now. It's poker night."

Mitch wasn't even going to ask. "What do you suggest then? What if I filled the radiator with some water?"

"Won't do any good. It'll just piss out of the hole. Your engine's so hot, probably been on the road some time now. You'd stall or blow your engine after two miles. That's my guess."

Mitch wanted to kick the truck. But he just stared at the ground trying to think of something. Every situation had a way out. Or at least he once thought so. Had once been trained to think so.

The old man left Mitch's side to take the hose out and replace the cap. "That'll be thirty three even," he said, returning to Mitch.

Mitch pulled out his wallet for the cash.

"You a cop?" the man asked when he noticed his badge in his wallet.

Mitch didn't know why he kept the thing. How many times had he thought about chucking it out the window the last ten hours, but could never bring himself to do it? No. That badge had been earned with his blood and guts. He may no longer be a cop, but he'd hold onto it.

"Not anymore, sir."

The man pointed to his leg. "Got injured on the job?"

"Yeah."

"Too bad. We could use a new sheriff in these parts."

Mitch smirked. "Sorry. Not interested."

"Now that's a damn shame," the old man said, the hopeful smile he held a moment ago now gone. "Tell you what. You look like an honest man. For a cop, that is."

"Ex-cop," Mitch reaffirmed.

The man waved his hand in the air. "Okay, ex-cop. Anyway, why don't you come home with me? The missus will take good care of you, give you a meal, fix up a bed for you for the weekend, until you get your truck fixed."

Mitch stared, not use to such hospitality. "That's very kind of you, sir."

"Name's Joe McFadden. Folks around here call me Ol' Joe. Not because of my age. Hell, I've still got a lot of years left. But because I've been in town for generations. Well, not me, but my family."

Mitch laughed. "I get the picture. I do appreciate the offer, but I have to decline. Can you give me directions to the mechanic? I'd like to see if I can catch him."

"I'm telling you it's pointless. He's closed up by now. But suit yourself. I doubt you'll even make it to town. You'll only end up having to sleep in this cramped truck all night. Probably wouldn't be a smart thing to do with that bum leg of yours. But get a pen and right down these directions."

Mitch did as instructed.

"You sure you want to risk driving instead of coming home with me? Your truck can be fixed first thing Monday morning when Maddy opens his shop."

"I'll be fine. Thanks again."

Mitch pulled out onto the road and followed Ol' Joe's directions. He'd beg the mechanic to fix his truck and offer him extra money if need be. But no way was Mitch bunking down with strangers, especially someone who would offer him food and comfort. He'd just left that behind with his family for Christ's sakes.

Per the instructions, he'd watch for the yellow tower and follow the road into town. Once his truck was repaired, he'd get directions to the nearest motel. In the morning, he'd drive again until he figured out what he wanted to do with his life now that his career was over.

About the author...

Award winning, multi-published author Christina James lives in a Massachusetts suburb with her two children. When penning stories, she enjoys writing of romance and heartache and of characters who overcome the odds. Passion is at the heart of every tale, and she strives to create realistic characters, so the reader can fall in love with them as much as she does. A sucker for a good love story, Christina writes hot, sensual romances with a little sarcastic wit and some humor in a contemporary setting. Look for her naughty Operation Series to continue featuring the other Navy SEALs. For naughty and wicked romance with no strings attached...read a Christina James novel.

Visit www.christinajamesauthor.com for excerpts and upcoming releases.

www.ingramcontent.com/pod-product-compliance
Lightning Source LLC
Chambersburg PA
CBHW070643130626
46555CB00006B/2683